P9-CCX-734

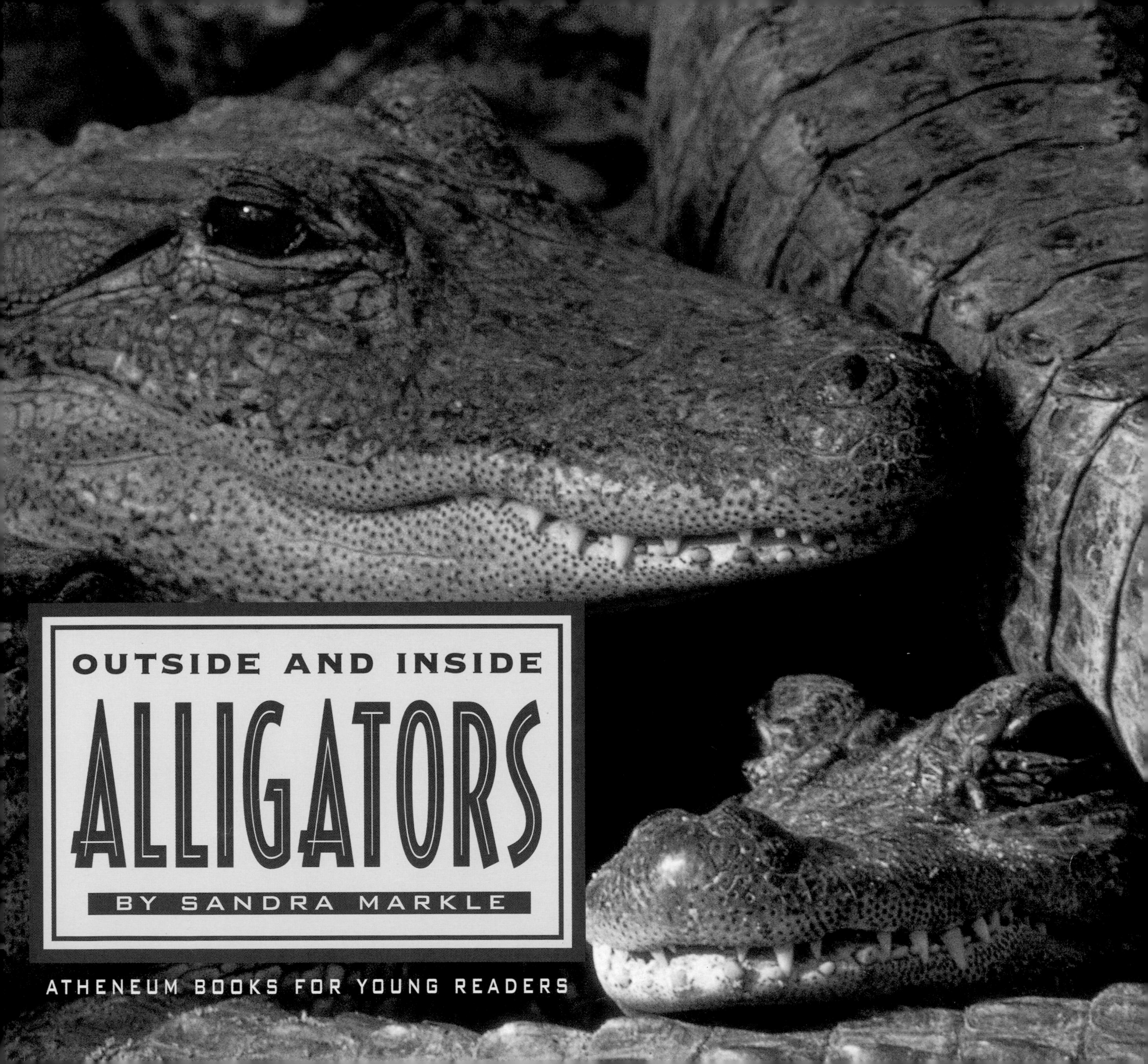
OUTSIDE AND INSIDE
ALLIGATORS
BY SANDRA MARKLE
ATHENEUM BOOKS FOR YOUNG READERS

For Yogi Gunther, the winner of my website's (www.compuquill.com) book award contest, and for Constance Parramore, with great appreciation for her help and friendship.

The author would like to thank the following for sharing their expertise and enthusiasm: Dr. Ruth M. Elsey, Wildlife Biologist, Louisiana Department of Wildlife and Fisheries; Dr. Howard Hunt, Zoo Atlanta; Walter Rhodes, South Carolina Department of Natural Resources; and Dr. Kent Vliet, University of Florida Department of Zoology.

ATHENEUM BOOKS FOR YOUNG READERS
An imprint of Simon & Schuster Children's Publishing Division
1230 Avenue of the Americas
New York, New York 10020

Book design by Anne Scatto/PIXEL PRESS
The text of this book is set in Melior
First Edition
Printed in Hong Kong
10 9 8 7 6 5 4 3 2 1
Library of Congress Cataloging-in-Publication Data:
Markle, Sandra.
Outside and Inside alligators / by Sandra Markle.—1st ed.
p. cm.
Summary: Describes the external and internal physical characteristics of alligators and how they find their food, mate, and raise their young.
ISBN 0-689-81457-7
1. Alligators—Juvenile literature. [1. Alligators.] I. Title.
QL666.C925M375 1998
597.98—dc21
97-39804 CIP AC

NOTE: To help readers pronounce words that may not be familiar to them, pronunciations are given in the glossary/index. Glossary words are italicized the first time they appear.

TITLE PAGE: *Group of young gators*

Alligators are amazing! They can swim swiftly despite their size and short, stubby legs. They can open their big mouths and grab *prey* underwater without getting any water in their *lungs* or *stomach.* How do they do that? And why does an alligator sometimes build a big mound of plants and mud and then guard it? This book will let you find out all these things and more. You'll even take a peek inside an alligator.

Alligators are only found in the southeastern United States and in China. Wherever they live, alligators spend a lot of time doing nothing—or so it seems. Lying around is really important for an alligator. The alligator on the facing page is nearly hidden, with just its *eyes* and *nostrils* above water. It is waiting to ambush a bird, a fish, a raccoon, a turtle, or even a deer that could become dinner. The same way you inflate a raft, the gator can take air into its lungs to make its big body float. It can submerge to any depth by controlling the amount of air. Because its nostrils, ears, and eyes are on top of its head, the alligator can have the rest of its body hidden and still breathe, hear, and look around.

Did you think this was an alligator? It's a close relative, a crocodile. Many kinds of crocodiles have longer, narrower snouts than alligators. Unlike most alligators, most crocodiles have one tooth on each side of the lower jaw that shows when their mouth is shut.

This alligator is lying around too, but the turtles are in no danger. The gator is not hunting. It is soaking up the sun's heat energy. After being in the sun for a while, the gator's body temperature will likely be about the same as yours. Usually, though, an alligator is cooler than you are. So, if you touch an alligator, it will feel cool.

Like you, an alligator has to be warm to be active and digest its food. Your body produces the heat it needs from the food you eat. But an alligator depends on soaking up this needed heat energy.

When you get too hot, you sweat. As this moisture evaporates, or changes to a gas, you feel cooler. An alligator cannot sweat. Instead, it exposes the moist inner surface of its mouth to the air for the same cooling effect. If the gator is still too hot, it moves into the shade or the water.

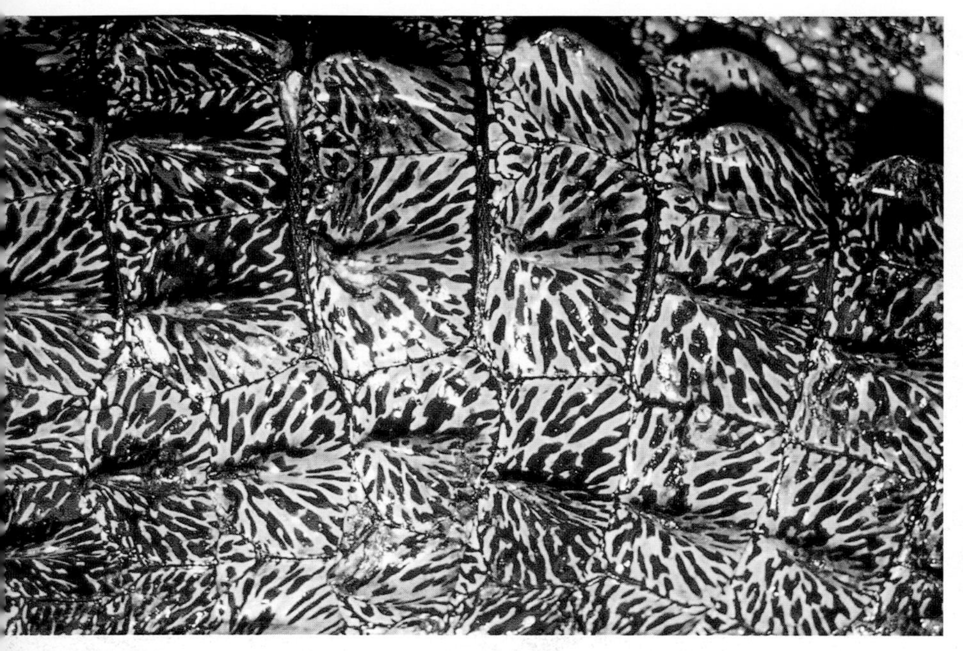

BODY SCALES

Scales on a gator's neck, back, and upper tail have a bony ridge.

BELLY SCALES

There is no bony ridge on the belly scales. This is the part sometimes made into leather.

Imagine how scratchy it would feel to crawl across the ground. An alligator's body is protected by a covering of large *scales*—like armor with stretchy skin in between—to allow the alligator to bend and twist. Some scales, such as the back scales, have embedded bony plates to make them even tougher.

Just as your skin continues to grow as you get bigger, an alligator's scales get bigger as it grows. Chinese alligators generally grow to be about as long as an average adult person. American alligators may grow bigger—as long as an average midsized car.

So what's under an alligator's skin? *Bones,* for one thing.

A building has a strong framework to support it and give it shape. An alligator's body, like yours, also has a framework—a bony *skeleton.* Do you wonder why there are so many different bones? This is because an alligator's body, like yours, can only bend where two bones meet. Just like having its body armor made up of lots of separate scales so it can move, having lots of bones makes an alligator flexible.

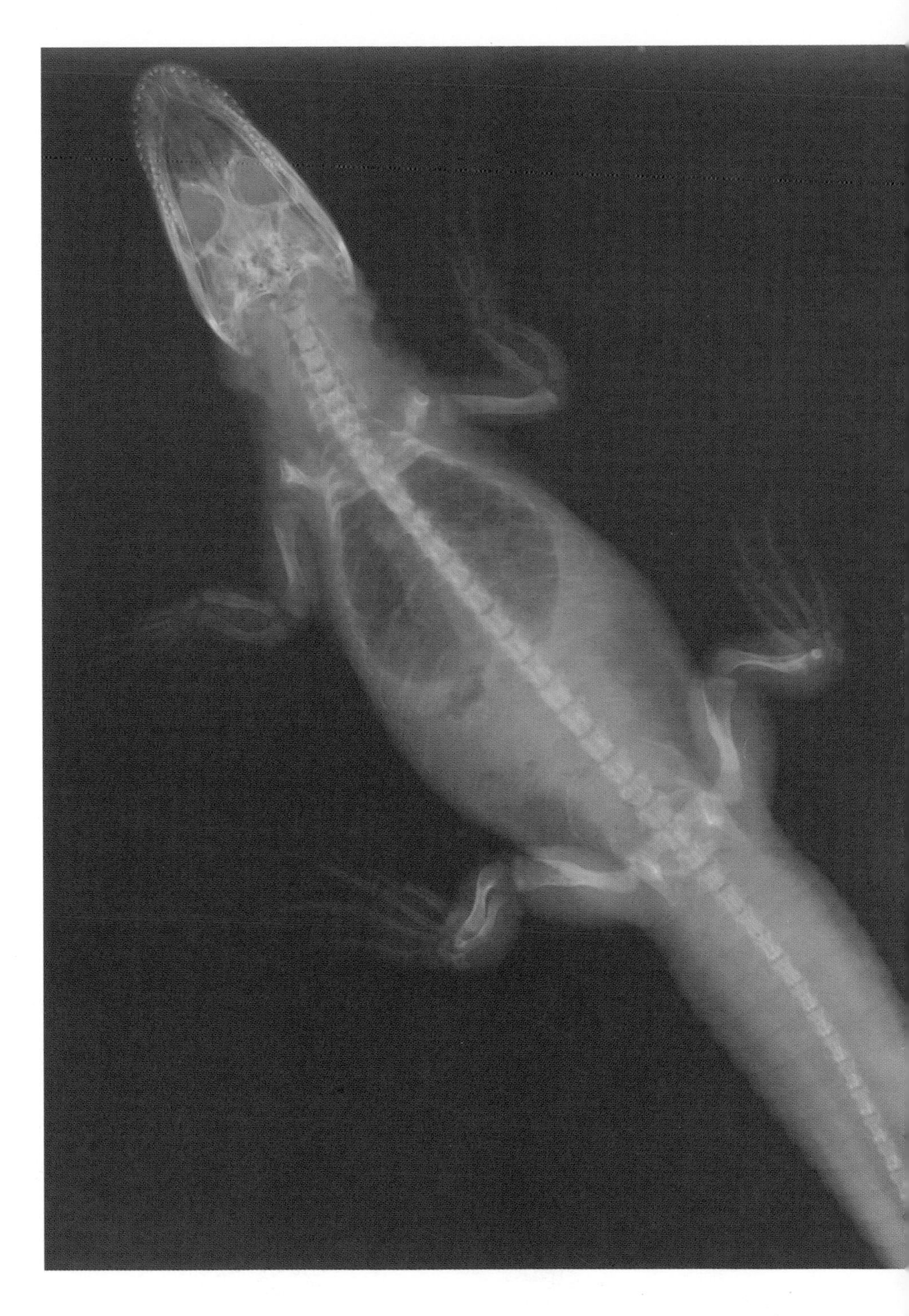

This is an X ray of an alligator's skeleton. Do you see its teeth?

The *skull* has to be very big. It is designed to support the alligator's big jaws.

Run your hand down the middle of your back. The bumps you feel are the bones of your spinal column. You have twenty-four back bones; an alligator has an average of sixty-five. About half of an alligator's spinal column is in its tail.

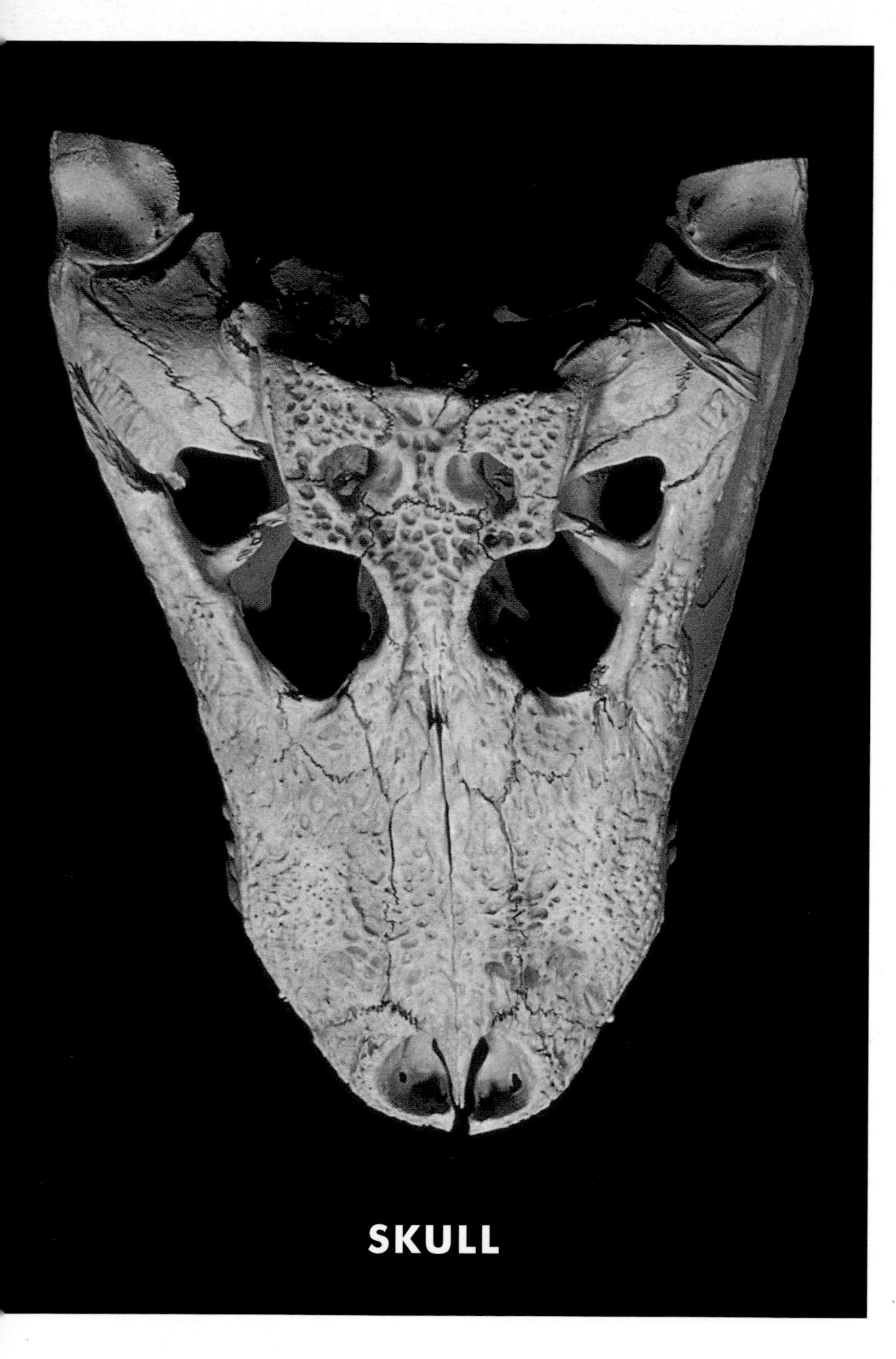

SKULL

BACK BONE

Is that big bulge on the alligator's neck fat or *muscle*?

Did you guess that the big bulge is a set of muscles that moves the alligator's jaws? Like yours, an alligator's jaws are bone. These bones, and all of the other bones, would not be able to move without muscles, body parts that pull on bones.

Muscles usually work in pairs. The muscles that close an alligator's mouth are big and strong. The muscles that open its mouth are much smaller and weaker.

Nick Clark of Gatorland in Florida says a three-to-four-meter (ten-to-twelve-foot) alligator can crush an adult turtle's shell in its jaws. He reports having seen an alligator with one bite snap in two a tree trunk about as big around as an adult man's fist. Nick says he sometimes shows that the muscles that open the mouth are weaker by holding the alligator's jaws shut. But he has to use two hands and a strong grip.

An alligator has to work hard to move across the land. Look at its short legs, bent close to its body. Usually, a gator crawls by twisting its body from side to side and "rowing" with its legs. Or, with a burst of energy, it can straighten its legs, push its belly off the ground, and walk. For a short distance, an alligator can even gallop fast enough to escape danger.

An alligator sheds its clumsiness when it slides into the water. It may paddle slowly with its feet, but to swim fast, it holds its legs close to its body. The torpedo-shaped gator slices through the water, propelled by powerful *S*-shaped sweeps of its long tail. Then the gator only has to kick its partly webbed hind feet to steer left or right.

An alligator's body is designed for hunting in water. A fleshy flap of skin at the back of the gator's mouth presses against a flap on the back of its big tongue. This creates a watertight valve so the alligator can open its mouth wide and grab prey underwater without gulping in water. Behind this valve, a separate tube lets air pass from the gator's nostrils to its lungs so it can continue to breathe.

Stick out your tongue and wiggle it. An alligator can't do that because its tongue is completely attached to the floor of its mouth.

When an alligator dives, its crescent-shaped nostrils close tight to keep water out of its lungs. Like you, an alligator needs *oxygen,* a gas in the air, to combine with food and generate energy. A gator's body, though, is able to use up energy very slowly. So, during a dive, its heart beats more slowly and some blood vessels get narrower. This slows the flow of blood to muscles and other parts that can make do with less oxygen, while a steady supply continues to the *brain* and *heart.* Making the most of its limited oxygen supply, a large alligator may stay submerged for more than an hour.

An alligator mainly hunts by sight, using its two eyes to judge the distance to its prey. During the attack, its eyes stay fixed on the target. Even when the gator lifts its head out of the water, muscles adjust the position of its eyeballs in their sockets so its view remains steady.

To keep its protruding eyes safe from struggling captured prey, the gator's eyes move down into their sockets when touched. As soon as the obstacle is gone, the eyes pop up again.

Alligators often hunt at night, so their eyes are designed to see well in dim light. Look at your eyes in a mirror. The dark spot in the center of your eye, the *pupil,* will appear bigger in dim light. It is like a window that lets light rays enter the eye. When the light rays entering the eye strike a light-sensitive layer called the *retina* at the back of the eye, signals are sent to the brain. Once the brain interprets these messages, you see. An alligator's slitlike pupil can open even wider than yours to let more light enter for better nighttime vision. Unlike you, an alligator also has a mirrorlike layer behind the retina which bounces light back onto the retina. This helps the gator take advantage of any light that is available.

See the alligator's third eyelid in the corner of its eye? This rolls over the eyes like goggles when it dives underwater. You can see that on page 14.

What a mouthful of teeth! Can you guess why this alligator has jerked its head up?

Did you guess that the alligator was tossing the fish up to make it fall down its throat? A gator has to swallow its food whole. Even though it has lots of teeth—from twenty to forty in each of its upper and lower jaws—an alligator can't chew. Its teeth are all cone-shaped and sharp for grabbing prey, and its jaws do not move sideways for grinding.

An alligator also loses its teeth easily. They are not firmly anchored into the gums the way your teeth are, so teeth may be lost when a prey struggles, or shed every year or two when they are worn. Luckily, underneath each tooth a new tooth is developing. It is these replacements just moving up that look like smaller teeth in an alligator's mouth. When an alligator is really old—more than thirty years —it often stops getting new teeth and may be nearly toothless.

Here is an alligator's stomach and the food it had recently eaten. Because an alligator does not chew up its food, the stomach has to do it. Alligators sometimes swallow hard objects such as stones, twigs, or even trash, like empty cans, to help this process. The food is mainly broken down, though, by special strong juices. Glands in the stomach lining pour these special juices onto the food. They help break down anything an alligator eats—even a prey animal's bones.

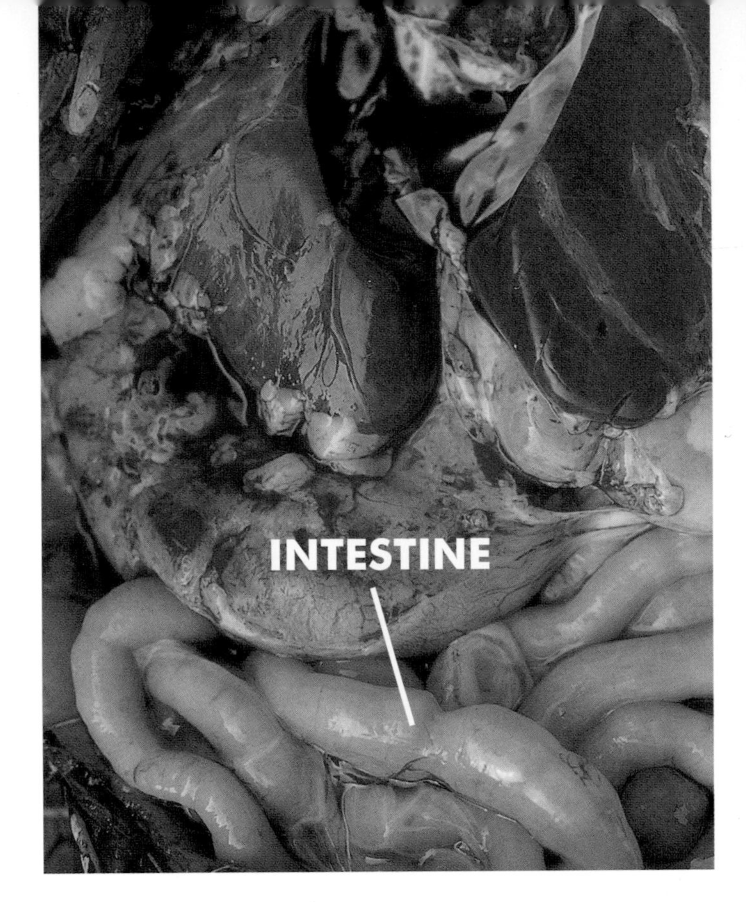

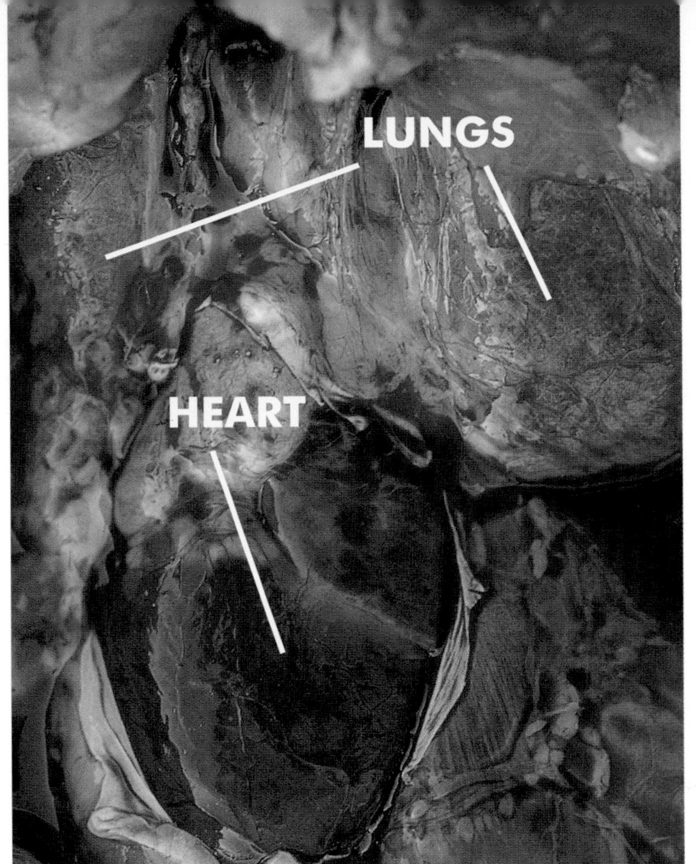

When the food is a soft, pulpy mass, the stomach's muscles push it into the *intestine.* There, more juices finish breaking it down into the five basic food *nutrients:* proteins, fats, carbohydrates, minerals, and vitamins. The alligator's body will use these to grow and be healthy. Wastes pass out an opening on the belly just in front of the tail. The nutrients pass through the walls of the intestine into the blood.

The heart pumps to push the blood along through the lungs and to all parts of the body. The lungs are like a sponge made up of many tiny bubblelike sacs that trap air. As the blood flows through the lungs, it picks up oxygen. *Carbon dioxide,* a waste gas given off when the body is active, is exchanged for the oxygen and returned to the lungs. Then the alligator breathes out this waste gas.

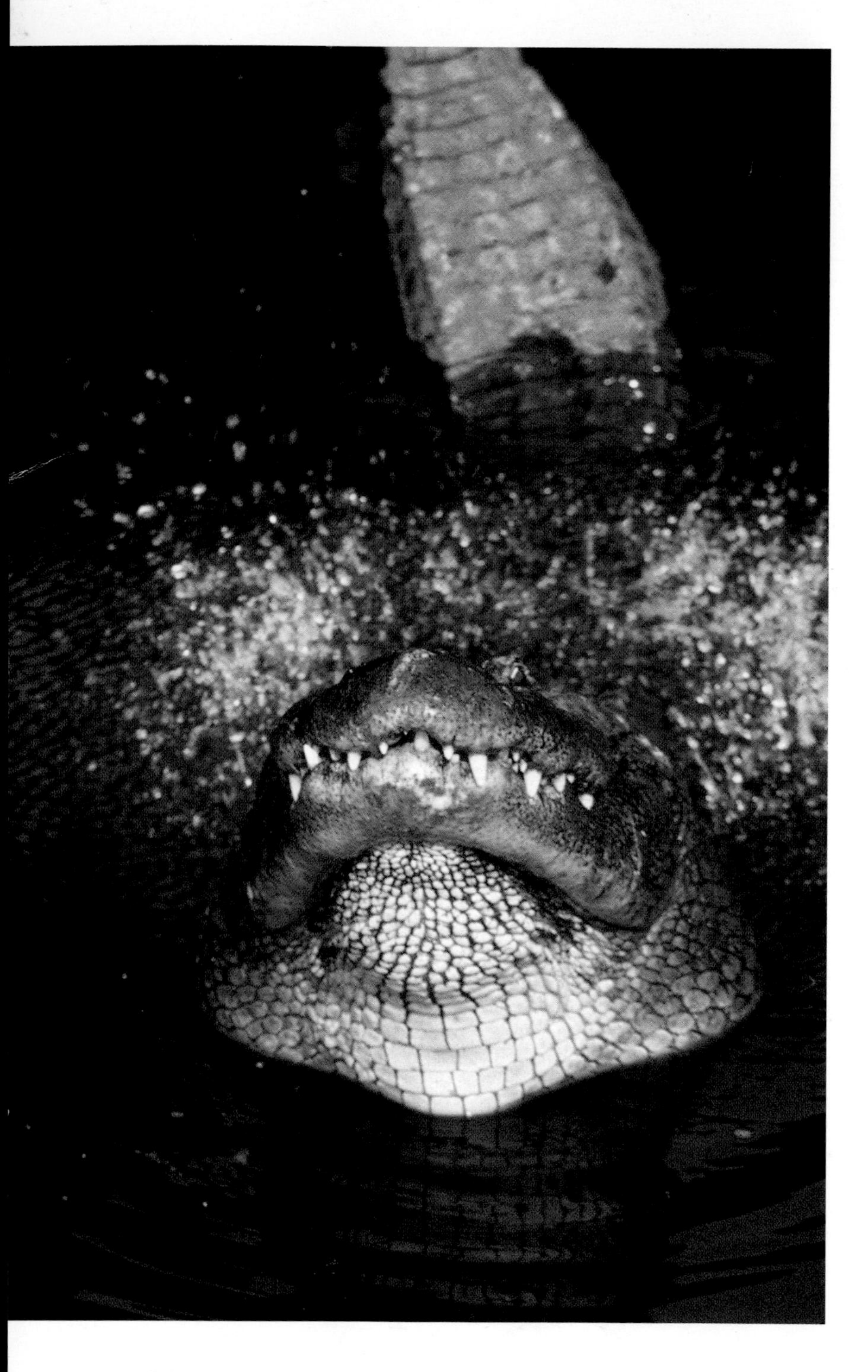

During the spring, adults gather in groups to find a mate. The bigger males may guard a mating territory. This male is creating a special effect called a water dance. By squeezing and releasing its chest and belly muscles underwater, the male is making the water appear to bubble up. The male also *bellows.* With its mouth closed, it blows out its breath in a series of thunderous blasts. Females bellow too. Alligators may also grunt or hiss. And courting couples often "talk" in softer sounds, such as purrs and coughs.

If another male approaches the couple, the two males will start to fight.

Here you can see the body part that produces *eggs* in a female's body. The eggs form and pass into the tube. When alligators mate, a cell from the male called a *sperm* joins with the female's egg in this tube. Then the cells at one spot on the egg divide and form the *embryo,* or young. The rest of the egg is the *yolk,* supplying food for the growing embryo.

Before the egg passes out of the tube, an eggshell surrounds it. This hard shell will protect the embryo developing inside. Because the shell is full of tiny holes, a steady supply of oxygen will also reach the growing baby.

Here you see a female crocodile laying her eggs. Female alligators lay their eggs the same way, but the alligator mother builds a *nest* using whatever material is available, usually leaves, twigs, and grass mixed with mud and sand. Working slowly over several days, she scrapes and digs mainly with her hind legs. Completed, the nest mound is the size of a big pile of leaves and packed pretty solidly. Next, she digs a hole in the top of the nest and deposits from twenty to fifty eggs in it. Then she crawls around the sides of the nest, pushing dirt over the eggs. Why do you suppose she does not crawl over the very top of the nest?

It takes the embryos from sixty-three to eighty-four days to be ready to hatch, depending on the temperature inside the nest. The embryos, like the adults, need heat from their surroundings for energy to grow and develop. But no matter how long it takes her offspring to develop, the female stays on guard. A female alligator usually builds her nest close to water. Then, even if she leaves to get something to eat, she does not need to go very far away.

This mother gator is removing a turtle from her nest. The Florida red-belly turtle came to lay her own eggs, but digging into the nest material could damage the gator eggs. This kind of turtle has an unusually hard shell—too hard for the alligator to crack. So the mother gator just carried the intruder away.

The mother alligator will also lunge to scare away enemies, such as raccoons or bears. Those animals would like to dig up an alligator-egg dinner.

Here you can see alligator embryos at three different stages of their development. The sixty-five-day-old embryo is nearly ready to hatch.

Walter Rhodes of the South Carolina Department of Natural Resources and Dr. Jeff Lang of the University of North Dakota are studying alligator embryo development. Dr. Lang discovered that nest temperature affects whether an embryo becomes a male or a female. Embryos that stay around 29° to 31.5°C (54° to 58.7°F) become females. Those that remain at 32.5° to 33°C (60.5° to 61.4°F) become males. At temperatures above 33°C (61.4°F), an increasing number of embryos become females.

Wonder where the heat that warms the embryos comes from? Researchers believe alligator eggs are warmed by the sun, by heat radiated from the ground beneath the nest, and by the rotting nest material. Like people huddling together to warm up, the growing embryos also share body heat, radiated through their eggshells. Because some embryos receive more heat than others, a *clutch* of eggs usually produces a mix of male and female alligators. Embryos that are too warm or too cool die.

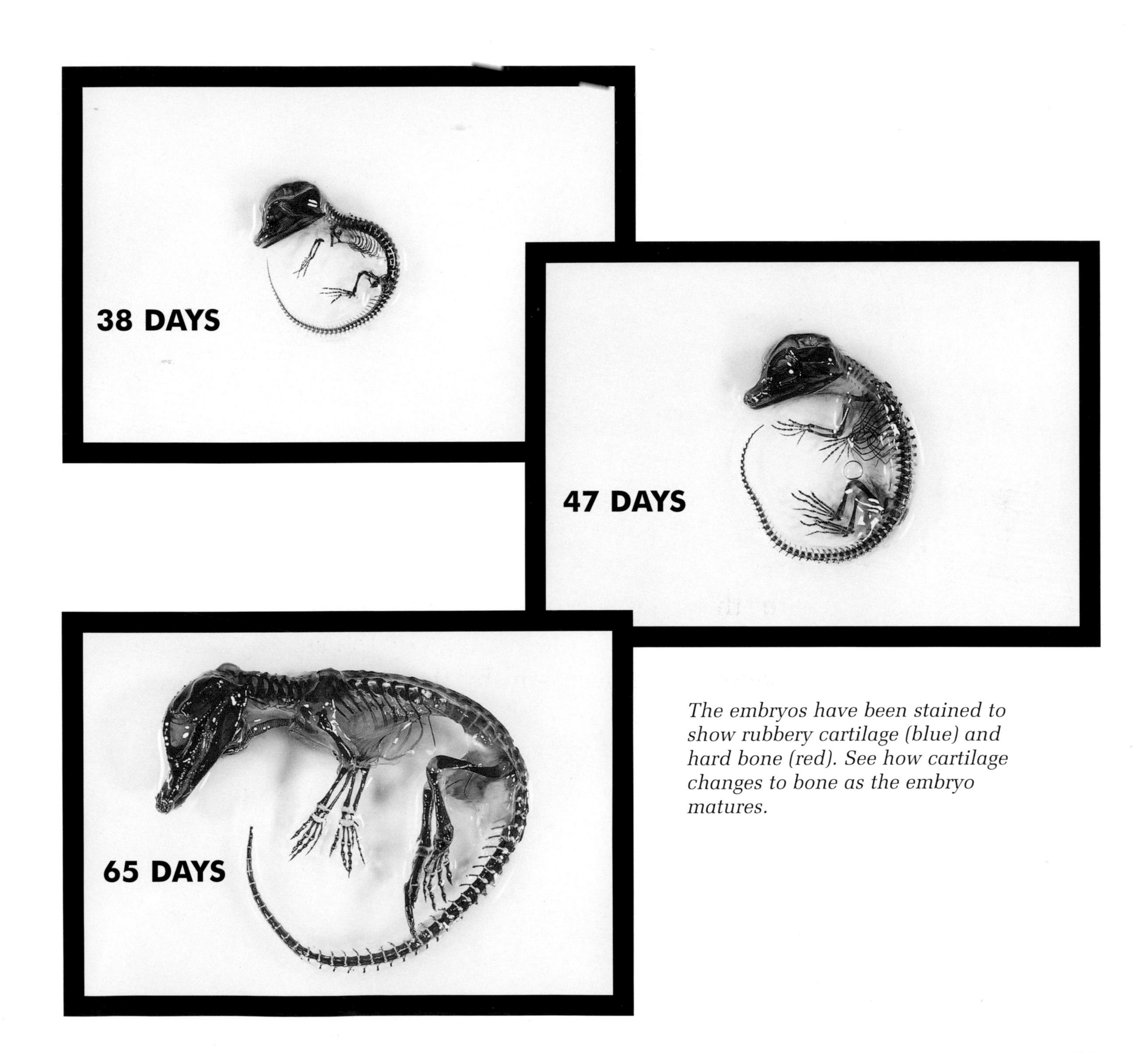

The embryos have been stained to show rubbery cartilage (blue) and hard bone (red). See how cartilage changes to bone as the embryo matures.

When baby alligators are ready to hatch, they yelp and grunt loudly enough for their mother to hear through the shell and the nest material. Mom scratches and bites to dig open the nest and uncover her eggs.

A baby alligator has a special scale that looks like a hard bump on the tip of its nose. The baby uses this scale to help pierce the tough inner *membrane* lining the egg and break out of the shell. This baby escaped on its own, but Mom may need to help out its brothers and sisters. She will crack any unopened eggs by picking them up and rolling them around in her mouth.

Once hatched, the babies head for the nearest water. Sometimes the mother gator gently carries her babies in her mouth and releases them into the water.

This baby alligator is sunning itself on Mom. The babies may stay near their mother for more than a year. While she does not really take care of them, she lets them stay and will attack to protect them.

This group is sharing its mother's private pool or gator hole. She dug and thrashed in the soft mud until she had a hole, which filled with rainwater. Because this private pool is so small, the gator hole heats up quickly and stays warm longer than any nearby body of water. Guarded by Mom, this makes a safe, warm nursery for the babies.

During a long, hot summer, gator holes may be the only source of water for many animals.

Eating lots of dragonflies, grasshoppers, crayfish, and small fish, this baby alligator will have enough energy to grow as much as one-third of a meter (about a foot) its first year.

Life is dangerous for a baby alligator. It spends much of its time hunting for food in shallow water. It has to stay alert for enemies, such as raccoons, turtles, big wading birds, and even large fish that would like to eat it. By the time it is two years old, the young alligator will be big enough to have fewer enemies. Then, when a newly hatched clutch of babies moves into the gator hole, the older alligator youngsters will go off on their own. Or they may be chased away by their mother.

With all of its body parts working together, the young alligator will try to stay safe and to find food. It will grow rapidly for the first five or six years and then continue growing slowly for the rest of its life. Clearly, alligators are special . . . from the inside out!

GLOSSARY/INDEX

BELLOW be-lō: Loud roaring noise made by both male and female alligators. This sound is made with the mouth closed by forcing air out in a series of blasts. **24**

BONES bōnz: The hard but lightweight parts that form a supporting frame for the alligator's body. **9-11**

BRAIN brān: Body part that receives messages about what is happening inside and outside the body and that sends messages to put the body into action. **17, 19**

CARBON DIOXIDE kär-bən dī-äk'-sīd: Gas that is given off naturally in body activities, carried to the lungs by the blood, and breathed out. **23**

CARTILAGE kär'-təl-ij: Lightweight, strong, rubbery material that forms an embryo's skeleton while it is developing. The cartilage is replaced by bone as the embryo matures. **31**

CLUTCH kləch: The group of eggs laid by one alligator mother. **30, 36**

EGG eg: Although the white, yolk, and shell are called the egg, the yolk is the real egg. The yolk is produced by the mother alligator's body. When joined by the sperm from the male alligator, the upper part of the yolk changes, growing into an embryo. The rest of the yolk supplies food for the embryo until it has developed enough to hatch. **26-27, 29-30, 33**

EMBRYO em-brē-ō: Name given to the developing young. **26, 28, 30**

EYE ī: Body part that lets the alligator see. An opening, the pupil, gets bigger or smaller to control the amount of light entering. Then a lens focuses light on the retina, triggering signals that travel to the brain. **5, 18, 19**

HEART härt: Body part that acts like a pump, constantly pushing blood throughout the alligator's body. **17, 23**

INTESTINE in-tes'-tən: The tube-shaped organ where food nutrients pass into the blood to be carried throughout the body. **23**

LUNG ləng: Body part where oxygen and carbon dioxide are exchanged inside tiny bubblelike air sacs. **3, 5, 16-17, 23**

MEMBRANE mem'-brān: The tough lining of the egg inside the shell. **33**

MUSCLE mə-səl: Body part that usually works in pairs. They move individual parts of the alligator's skeleton by pulling on them from opposite sides. **11-12, 17**

NEST nest: The mound of mud and plant material that the mother alligator piles up and then digs into to lay her eggs. The embryos depend on the heat radiated from this material to develop. **27, 29, 33**

NOSTRILS näs-trəlz: Two crescent-shaped openings on the top of the alligator's nose. These can close to keep water from getting into the alligator's lungs when it dives. **5, 16, 17**

NUTRIENTS nü'-trē-əntz: Chemical building blocks into which food is broken down for use by the alligator's body. **23**

OXYGEN äk'-si-jən: A gas in the air that is breathed into the lungs, carried by the blood to all the body parts, and combined with food nutrients to release energy. **17, 23, 26**

PREY prā: The food the alligator catches and eats. **3, 16, 18, 22, 35**

PUPIL pyu'-pəl: Opening in the eye that lets light enter. **19**

RETINA re-tən-ə: Layer at the back of the eye that is light-sensitive. When light strikes it, messages are sent to the brain. The brain figures out these messages, and the alligator sees. **19**

SCALES skālz: Places where the skin is thicker for extra protection. **8, 33**

SKELETON ske-lə-tən: Framework of bones that supports the body and gives it its shape. **9**

SKULL skəl: The name used to describe all of the bones that form the head. **10**

SPERM spərm: The cell produced by the male alligator. When the sperm joins with the female's egg, an embryo develops. **26**

STOMACH stə-mək: Stretchy body part able to store and break down food before it enters the intestine. **3, 22**

TOOTH tüth: Body part used for getting food. Each tooth is cone-shaped and sharp for grabbing and holding on to food. New teeth form underneath to replace teeth that are lost. **21**

YOLK yōk: Food supply for the developing baby alligator. **26**

ä as in cart   ā as in ape   ə as in banana   ē as in even   ī as in bite
ō as in go   ü as in rule   ʉ as in fur

LOOKING BACK

1. Check out the alligator's big mouth on the cover. How many teeth can you see? Do you remember how many teeth an alligator is likely to have? If not, check back on page 21.
2. Check out the alligator's front foot on page 11. Three of the five toes have claws. The clawed toes help the alligator dig.
3. Take another look at page 18. You may be surprised to learn that alligators actually help their bird neighbors. While the alligators sometimes eat a young bird that falls out of a tree, they also eat raccoons, rats, and snakes that would otherwise eat the birds' eggs.
4. Take another look at the eggshell on page 32. The shell is thickest when it is first laid, and then it slowly thins as the embryo develops. A thinner shell lets more oxygen enter the egg to meet the growing baby's needs.
5. Compare the color of the baby gator on page 36 to the adult on page 5. The baby alligator's stripes help it hide among plants in shallow water. Do you remember how adult alligators hide? If not, check back on page 5.

PHOTO CREDITS

COVER:	© Rich Kirchner
TITLE PG:	© Jeff Foott
p. 3	© Rich Kirchner
p. 4	© Erwin and Peggy Bauer
p. 5	Kent Vliet
p. 7	© Tom and Pat Leeson
p. 8	Kent Vliet (both)
p. 9	© 1997 Busch Entertainment Corporation. All rights reserved.
p. 10	© Joe McDonald, Chris Brochu
p. 11	© Tom and Pat Leeson
p. 13	Ruth Elsey
p. 14	Kent Vliet
p. 16	© Tom and Pat Leeson; Kent Vliet
p. 17	© Doug Perrine, Innerspace Visions
p. 18	© Erwin and Peggy Bauer
p. 19	Ruth Elsey
p. 20	© Rich Kirchner
p. 21	Ruth Elsey
p. 22	Ruth Elsey
p. 23	Ruth Elsey (both)
p. 24	Kent Vliet
p. 25	Chris Brochu
p. 26	Ruth Elsey
p. 27	Kent Vliet
p. 28	Ruth Elsey
p. 29	Howard Hunt
p. 30-31	Hans Larson
p. 32	Ruth Elsey
p. 34	Howard Hunt
p. 35	© Rich Kirchner
p. 36	Kent Vliet
p. 37	© Rich Kirchner